Wallace, Barbara Brooks
Argyle

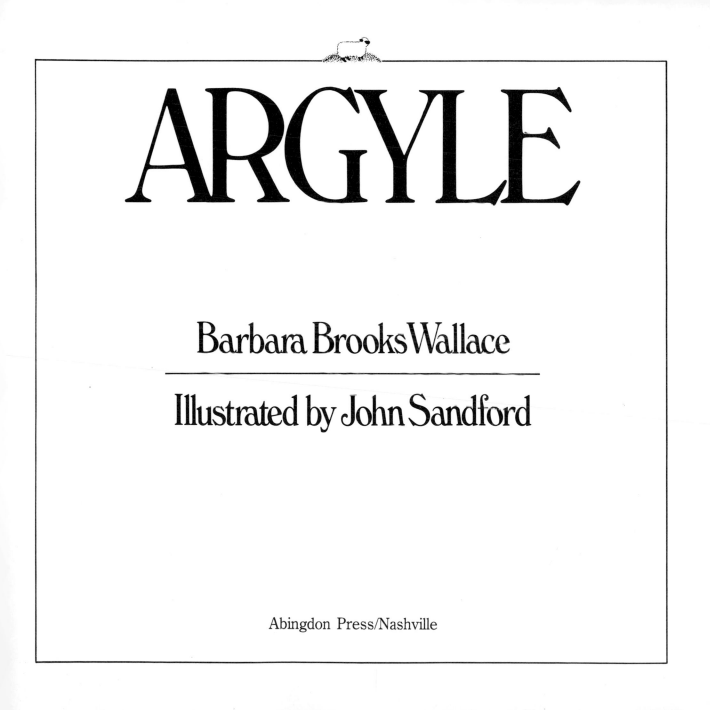

ARGYLE

Barbara Brooks Wallace

Illustrated by John Sandford

Abingdon Press/Nashville

For
JIMMY of CLAN WALLACE
with love and the usual ten

ARGYLE

Text Copyright © 1987 by Barbara Brooks Wallace
Illustrations Copyright © 1987 by Abingdon Press

All Rights Reserved

BOOK DESIGN BY JOHN R. ROBINSON

This book is printed on acid-free paper.

Library of Congress Cataloging-in-Publication Data

Wallace, Barbara Brooks, 1922-
    Argyle.

    Summary: A Scottish sheep's unusual diet causes
him to produce multicolored wool, which changes
his life and the fortunes of his owners.
    [1. Sheep—Fiction. 2. Scotland—Fiction]
I. Sandford, John, 1948-   ill. II. Title.
PZ7.W1547Ar   1987   [Fic]   87-1369

        ISBN 0-687-01724-6 (alk. paper)

PRINTED IN HONG KONG

Once upon a time, somewhere in Scotland, there was a sheep whose name was Argyle.

Argyle was exactly like all the other sheep. He looked like a sheep, and he felt like a sheep. He liked to do the same things other sheep did. He wasn't one bit different from any of them, and he didn't give a *hoot mon* about it.

When MacDougal the sheepherder herded his sheep into the pen to shear their wool for market, he couldn't tell Argyle from the rest of them.

"A sheep is a sheep," MacDougal always said. "They're all the same."

That was all right with Argyle. It was exactly the way he wanted it.

All day with the rest of MacDougal's sheep, Argyle roamed the highlands and the lowlands and the middle lands. It was peaceful and quiet. It was exactly the way he wanted it.

Sheep like to go around in bunches. So did Argyle. But once in a while a sheep likes to wander away from the others. So did Argyle. He didn't do it very often. Just sometimes.

One day he wandered off and came
to a place behind some tall rocks where
he had never been before. The grass
there tasted really good. So did some
strange little flowers with red and blue
and white and green and purple and
yellow petals. In fact, they were
outstanding.

Argyle didn't tell anyone about them.
But the next day he quietly wandered
back. And the day after that. And the
day after that. He ate hundreds of the
little colored flowers.

One day MacDougal's wife,
Katharine, said, "Why dinna ye tell me
about the many-colored sheep,
MacDougal?"

"Because we do na have a many-
colored sheep, Katharine," said
MacDougal.

"Look again," said Katharine.

MacDougal looked again and saw that they did indeed have a many-colored sheep. Its wool was red and blue and white and green and purple and yellow. The sheep was Argyle.

MacDougal ran for his shears and started clipping. Katharine ran for her knitting needles and started knitting.

Then they both ran to show all their friends and neighbors the socks Katharine had knit. They were a beautiful plaid. Well! You can imagine what a sensation a sheep who grew wool that knit into *plaid* socks would be in Scotland. Argyle became famous overnight.

It didn't take MacDougal long to decide that Argyle should not be wandering around with the rest of the sheep, so he put Argyle in a pen by himself where he was all alone. Except for the hundreds of people who paid a lot of money to come and see him. And to buy some of his wool. They paid a lot of money for that, too. Soon MacDougal and Katharine grew very rich. Mayor Loch of Lomond came out and gave Argyle a medal.

But Argyle felt as if he weren't a sheep anymore. He was just a public exhibition. He hated it. It was never peaceful and quiet. He couldn't roam the highlands and the lowlands and the middle lands. And, of course, he couldn't get back to the place where the pretty little colored flowers grew. So he started to turn sheep color again.

MacDougal was so worried that he fed Argyle all kinds of vitamins and minerals and terrible-tasting food. It made Argyle miserable.

Soon he not only stopped *feeling* like a sheep, he stopped *looking* like one, too, because all his wool fell out. Well! It didn't take long for the people to stop coming around. Except for Mayor Loch of Lomond, who came to take away the medal.

Fortunately, he couldn't take away MacDougal's money, so MacDougal and Katharine stayed rich the rest of their days. Katharine kept right on knitting and finally discovered a way to make plaid socks out of different bits of dyed wool. She called them Argyle socks, of course. You may have heard of them.

MacDougal finally gave up on Argyle and sent him out with the rest of the sheep. Argyle grew back his old sheep coat, and soon you couldn't tell him from any other sheep. He looked like a sheep and he felt like a sheep again.

As for the place with the pretty colored flowers, if Argyle ever went back there, he never told anyone. And he stayed his plain old sheep color, so you could be pretty sure he wasn't eating anything but the grass.

He just roamed the highlands and the lowlands and the middle lands with all the other sheep. It was peaceful and quiet. It was exactly the way he wanted it.

Gumption!

by **Elise Broach**

with pictures by

Richard Egielski

Atheneum Books for Young Readers

New York London Toronto Sydney

Uncle Nigel was Peter's favorite uncle.

He was loud.

He was brave.

He was funny.

And he always let Peter stay up too late.

So when Uncle Nigel invited Peter to join him on

an expedition to Africa, there was no question

what Peter would say.

On their first morning at Wanabutu Adventure Camp, Uncle Nigel said to Peter, "I'm going to make a real explorer out of you, my boy! Today we will search for that rarest and wildest of beasts: the Zimbobo Mountain Gorilla."

"Wow!" Peter cried. "The Zimbobo Mountain Gorilla! Do you think we'll find one?"

Uncle Nigel patted Peter's head. "Never know, lad. The jungle is full of surprises. Now, tally ho! It's a good five miles up that mountain."

With long strides and swinging arms, Uncle Nigel led the way.
Peter ran to keep up.

They came to a dense thicket.

"Uncle Nigel," Peter said, "I can't get through."

Uncle Nigel winked. "Nonsense, my boy! All it takes is a bit
of gumption." He took out his hunting knife and hacked his way
through the fat, prickly leaves.

Peter tried to follow.

Uncle Nigel stopped in his tracks.

"I say!" he cried. "Snake skin!"

He tapped a tree. "Hmmm. There are snakes here somewhere. Sly ones. Look sharp, Peter."

"I will," Peter promised.

Soon they came to a sun-scorched plain.

"Uncle Nigel," Peter said, "I'm hot. I need a rest."

Uncle Nigel smiled. "Nonsense, my boy! All it takes is a bit of gumption." He took a long swig from his canteen and strode through the tall grass.

Peter tried to follow.

Uncle Nigel stopped in his tracks. "I say! Elephant dung!"

He lifted his binoculars and peered in every direction. "Hmmm. There are elephants here somewhere. Big ones. Watch your step, Peter."

"I will," Peter promised.

Then they came to a deep river.

"Uncle Nigel," said Peter, "I can't cross that."

Uncle Nigel grinned. "Nonsense, my boy! All it takes is a bit of gumption." He took a life vest out of his pack and plunged into the dark water.

Peter tried to follow.

Uncle Nigel stopped in his tracks. "I say!

Crocodile eggs!"

He dug at the ground with his boot. "Hmmm.

There are crocs here somewhere. Hungry ones.

Stay close, Peter."

"I will," Peter promised.

At last they were deep in the heart of the jungle. They began the long climb up the mountain. The ground was rocky and steep.

"Uncle Nigel," Peter said, "I can't climb all the way to the top."

Uncle Nigel laughed. "Nonsense, my boy! All it takes is a bit of gumption." He took a rope from his pack, threw it over a tree branch, and pulled himself up the slope.

Peter tried to follow.

Uncle Nigel stopped in his tracks. "I say! Footprints! That's ace, lad! The footprints of the Zimbobo Mountain Gorilla!"

"Wow," said Peter.

Uncle Nigel tapped a tree.

He lifted his binoculars and peered in every direction.

He dug at the ground with his boot.

Then he shook his head. "Hmmm. Nothing. I expect we gave them a fright and they legged it."

"Uncle Nigel—"

"Not to worry, Peter! Just think: We're standing in the home of that rarest and wildest of beasts . . ."

"The Zimbobo Mountain Gorilla," said Peter.

Uncle Nigel sighed. "I'm sorry we didn't see one, my boy. But that's what you learn as a real explorer: You might not find what you're after, but it's always worth the trip." He looked at Peter. "Bit disappointed, are you, lad?"

"Oh, no, Uncle Nigel . . . the jungle is amazing!"

"That's the spirit! Are you zonked? Need a break? It's a good five miles back to camp."

"No, Uncle Nigel. I can do it." Peter grinned. "All it takes is a bit of gumption."

Uncle Nigel thumped Peter on the shoulder. "Jolly good, Peter! Down the mountain we go. And don't worry, old sport . . . we'll try again tomorrow."

For my wonderful friend Claire Streeter Carlson,
a guaranteed source of laughter,
misadventures, and gumption—E. B.

For Dave, Les, and Ed, the gumption guys—R. E.

Atheneum Books for Young Readers
An imprint of Simon & Schuster Children's Publishing Division
1230 Avenue of the Americas, New York, New York 10020
Text copyright © 2010 by Elise Broach
Illustrations copyright © 2010 by Richard Egielski
Book design by Ann Bobco and Michael McCartney
The text for this book is set in Matchwood Bold.
The illustrations for this book are rendered
in ink, pens, and watercolor on paper.
Manufactured in China
First Edition
2 4 6 8 10 9 7 5 3 1
Library of Congress Cataloging-in-Publication Data
Broach, Elise.
Gumption! / Elise Broach ; illustrated by Richard Egielski. — 1st ed.
p.   cm.
Summary: When Peter goes on an African adventure with his beloved Uncle Nigel,
who hopes to spot a rare gorilla, the oblivious Nigel urges Peter on by telling him
to have gumption, while Peter keeps his eyes open and uses his ingenuity.
ISBN: 978-1-4169-1628-4
[1. Perseverance (Ethics)—Fiction. 2. Adventure and adventurers—Fiction. 3. Uncles—Fiction.
4. Jungle animals—Fiction. 5. Africa—Fiction.] I. Egielski, Richard, ill. II. Title.
PZ7.B78083Gum 2010 [E]—dc22 2008049048